Don't Make Me Laugh, Liam

Also in the Totally Tom series:

Limited

TOTALLY TOM

Don't Make Me Laugh, Liam

Jenny Oldfield

illustrated by
Neal Layton

Hodder
Children's
Books

a division of Hodder Headline Limited

One

'What d'you get if you pour boiling water down a rabbit hole?' Liam asked Tom.

'I dunno. What d'you get if you pour boiling water down a rabbit hole?'

'Hot cross bunnies!' Liam doubled up laughing. 'Get it? Hot cross bunnies!'

Tom grinned.

'OK, then. What d'you call an egg with swollen glands?' Liam slid down the banister and landed in the hall.

Tom watched from the landing. 'I dunno. What d'you call an egg with swollen glands?'

'Humpty Mumpty!' Liam cried. 'Humpty Mumpty. Mumps. Humpty Dumpty. Get it?'

Tom slid down the stairs to join him.

'How many times have I told you not to slide down the banister, Tom Bean!' his mum called out from the kitchen.

Whizz–'Ouch!' Tom gasped as he landed. 'Right. Where d'you take a sick frog?' he challenged.

'I dunno. Where d'you take a sick frog?' Liam said in his cool accent. He picked up Tom's skateboard and inspected the stickers.

Tom came in quick and super-slick with his answer. 'To the hop-ital!'

'What's worse than a giraffe with a sore throat?' Liam shot back.

'I dunno. What's worse...?'

'A centipede with blisters on his feet!' Liam crowed. He burst through the front door, slammed down the board then skated off down the garden path.

Tom grabbed his baseball cap and his second best board, then shot off after his cousin.

'Boys, it's time for...tea!' Beth Bean called after them.

Rrrrrr-clink-click-rrrr! Their trucks whirred off along the street.

'And it's Liam Bean pulling a slappy on to the kerb, and into a phat Smithgrind, building up speed into a crooked grind... wowee!'

'Wicked!' Tom cried. He grinned at Liam's gabbled voice-over. 'Tom Bean follows with a combination of ollies to go-go-go!'He ollies up onto the kerb, then swivels his upper body, allowing his lower body and board to follow. Now his back foot has become his leading foot...yeah, Tom lands and rides out fakie into the park entrance!'

Liam finished his commentary on Tom's slick move. He'd picked up his deck and

stood waiting for his cousin by the
stone gateposts.

'Come and meet the gang,' Tom invited,
happy to introduce Liam to Wayne, Ryan,
Kalid, Lola and Kingsley.

'Hey, you lot, keep the noise down!'
Angry Dad from Tom's road yelled from
outside his house.

'Live to skate, dude!' Kingsley cried,
rocking his board on the lip of the coping
of the main ramp in the park. 'Yo, wicked!'

As the main man rocked and rolled, Kalid
pulled a backside pop shove-it, while Lola,
Wayne and Ryan pulled slappies and
feebles on a low kerb.

'Well cool!' Liam grinned. Soon he was in
the centre of the action, pulling a gnarly
stalefish which sent him turning 180 and
brought him smoothly down the ramp.

'Wow, nice air!' Lola gasped.

'Yeah, moves don't come much radder
than that!' Ryan agreed.

Everyone smacked their decks on the

ground in a round of applause.

'Who's that?' Kingsley asked.

'That's Liam. He's my cousin from Dublin,' Tom answered proudly.

'I'm well impressed,' Kingsley admitted. He pulled a metre-high acid drop from the side edge of the ramp and went to join the new kid.

'Hey, Liam,' he grunted.

Liam picked up his board. 'Howya,' he replied.

Kingsley looked the newcomer up and down. He was small and skinny like Tom, with the same wide grin. In fact, Tom and Liam could be brothers. Liam wore the right logo on his shirt and big name trainers. 'Yo, dude!' Kingsley made a high-five. 'Welcome to Hammett Park skate gang!'

'Liam, welcome to Woodbridge Junior School.' Mr Wright made Tom's cousin feel at home. He gave him a seat next to Tom and made a point of asking about where he came from and why he was here.

'Sir, I'm Irish,' Liam answered politely.

'I think we've gathered that,' Leftie chuckled. 'And what's the reason for your visit to England?'

'Sir, my mam has to go to a wake in London. It's my great uncle Michael that died.'

'I'm sorry to hear that,' Leftie sympathised.

'Ah no, they'll have a great crack,' Liam told him cheerfully. 'The whole family will be there. Uncle Michael was eighty. He wouldn't want any tears.'

'And it's nice for Tom to have you around, I'm sure.'

'Yessir!' Tom confirmed.

'Hmm. Double trouble!' Bex Stevens muttered to her buddy, Danielle Hazelwood. Bex had already noted the similarity between the cousins. 'How much d'you bet that anything Tom Bean can do, Liam can do worse!'

7

Unluckily for her, Liam overheard the snide remark.

'Right, everyone, time to get changed for PE,' the teacher instructed. 'We'll be outdoors in the playground, playing rounders. Everyone report to me in T-shirts and shorts in five minutes, no messing!'

'What's rounders?' Liam asked, wriggling into a spare pair of Tom's shorts in the boys' changing room.

'It's where you whack a ball with a thing like a baseball bat and run like mad to get round the pitch,' Kalid explained. 'The bowler bowls underarm, so it's easy peasy.'

'Let's go!' livewire Liam exclaimed.

So Ryan led the charge out to the playground, arms outstretched, doing his usual fighter pilot impression with arms wide and a loud 'Neee-yah-boom!'.

Soon Leftie had organised the teams and the game began.

'And it's Lola pitching for the Reds.

Ace striker Kingsley whacks the ball to
the outfield for the Blues!' Tom ran the
commentary in a high-pitched, excited
voice. He watched Kingsley's long legs cover
the ground while Danielle made a feeble
attempt to field the ball for the Reds.

'Rounder!' the Blues cried as Kingsley
completed the circuit.

'Nice hit, Kingsley!' Leftie noted.

Now it was Liam's turn to hit the hot spot, with Bex bowling for the Reds.

But this was a different Bex to the normal neat and petite, annoyingly sensible and grown-up teacher's pet. This was Bex the Cunning Competitor, Bex the Beast!

'Watch her, she cheats!' Ryan whispered.

Liam stood ready, holding the bat high, a bundle of energy ready to unleash itself.

Bex narrowed her eyes and bowled deliberately wide.

Liam hit out at the ball, spun round on the spot and almost fell over. 'Hmph!'

'She did that on purpose to put you off!' Ryan warned.

'No-ball!' Leftie ruled.

So Bex took up position with a second attempt. This time she made a neat dummy move, then quickly released an unexpected throw.

'Cheat!' Ryan, Kalid and Wayne cried.

Caught out by the dummy, Liam swung wildly at the ball, which caught the

edge of his bat and plopped tamely to
the ground.

'Run!' Tom yelled. 'Get to first base!'

But Bex was in, quick as a whippet,
fielding the ball and chucking it to Sasha,
who guarded first base. Sasha tipped the
post with the ball and Liam was given out.

'Bummer!' Tom sighed. Liam shrugged
and sat out, quietly planning his revenge.

'Five rounders to the Blues!' Leftie
announced, when all their batters were out.

A hot and sweaty Blue team handed the
bats over to the Reds.

'Here, have this one.' Liam generously
offered his bat to the player who had
bowled him out.

Bex took it and rushed to the hot spot,
the first to bat for the Reds.

'Bags I bowl!' Liam jumped in with a
gleam in his eye.

'What's he up to?' Wayne whispered
to Tom.

'Dunno.' Definitely something,

but what?

They watched as Liam built up to a mega-fast throw.

Zoom! The ball flew through the air.

Whizz! Bex swung the bat.

Prrroooop! The ball made contact with the bat, the bat twisted wildly in Bex's grip, she lost hold of the handle and it flew up to the sky, while the ball did a slow,

graceful arc in the air.

'Catch it!' Kalid cried to Tom at first base.

Tom ran forward and made an easy catch. Meanwhile, the bat rocketed on like a guided missile to reach the outer field.

'Oh no!' Danielle and the rest of the Reds groaned as their star hitter was given out.

The bat finally landed with a clunk on the tarmac and rolled down the steps into the caretaker's basement.

'Wrrrufff!' A roar from the cellar told the players that Fat Lennox had sunk his teeth into the stray missile.

'How?' Kingsley stood with his mouth open in amazement as Liam trotted to rejoin the Blues. 'What happened? How did you do that?'

Liam winked and chuckled. He drew a small tub of hair gel from his shorts pocket and held it up. 'It's good for making stuff slippy,' he explained. 'After I smeared it on the handle of Bex's bat, she'd got no chance of scoring a rounder!'

'Cool!' Kalid breathed.

'Not fair!' Bex whimpered, discovering the smelly gel on the palms of her hands. She was about to run and dob Liam in until Lola stood in her way.

'Don't even think about it,' she warned. 'Or else I'll tell Mr Wright that you let Sasha borrow your Maths homework on condition that she let you copy her English!'

Silence from Miss Squeaky Clean.

Grins all round for the Blues.

'What's this stuff like on your hair?' Tom asked Liam, taking the plastic tub and sniffing warily.

'Rotten!' Liam confessed. 'But it's wicked for most other things. You should try it some time!'

Two

'Knock, knock.'

  'Who's there?'

  'Jess.'

  'Jess who?'

  'Jess me.'

  Tom groaned over his Rice Crispies.

  'Knock, knock.' Quickfire Liam rollicked on.

  'Who's there?'

'Sonia.'

'Sonia who?'

'Sonia foot, I can smell it from here.'

'Ergh!' Tom wrinkled his nose. 'OK then– why doesn't Dracula have any friends?'

'Because he's a real pain in the neck!' Liam stole the punchline and was about to launch into another knock-knock joke when Beth cut in.

'Your mum's on the phone,' she told Liam. 'Have a quick word with her before you set off for school.'

'You wanna know what Liam did to Bex Stevens in rounders yesterday?' Tom asked his big brother, Nick.

'Nope.'

Tom told him all about it anyway, including how Lennox had charged out of the cellar with the bat between his teeth, and how Bernie King, the caretaker, had banned them from playing rounders in the playground for the rest of the term.

'Even though Leftie was there,' Tom

complained. 'Bernie marched straight off to Waymann's office and said that rounders bats were a danger to people's health and they should be stopped.'

'Fat Lennox is a danger to people's health,' Nick mumbled, remembering the dog from his own days at Woodbridge Juniors.

For once, he and Tom agreed.

'Why does a lion have a fur coat?' Liam had finished his phone call and burst back into the kitchen with another joke for Tom.

'Give it a rest,' Nick pleaded.

'Because he'd look stupid in a plastic mac!' Liam crowed.

Then, before anyone could even groan, he slapped his baseball cap down over his half-drunk glass of orange juice on the breakfast table.

'Betcha I can drink that juice without touching the hat!' he challenged.

'Zzzzz!' Nick snored.

'Betcha can't!' Tom shot back.

'OK, then, watch me!' Liam ducked under the table and made loud slurping noises. Then he sprang out, his face covered in triumph. 'See, told ya I could!'

'No way!' Giving a weary sigh. Nick lifted the cap from the glass. Sure enough, the juice was still there.

'Ha!' Liam laughed, grabbing the glass and slurping for real. 'Told ya I could do it!'

'Ha-blinkin'-ha!' Nick said in a dis-chuffed voice. 'My sides ache from laughing. I thought Tom was bad, but you're way ahead in the annoying-little-brat league.'

'Hey, thanks!' Liam grinned. Big compliment!

'School, you two!' Beth ordered, thrusting Tom's bag at him and shoving him and Liam out of the door. 'And, if it's not asking for miracles, will you try and get through a whole day without landing in trouble!'

'Look at this!' Tom invited Wayne during the art lesson that afternoon.

Liam had already made the whole class fall about with his knock-knock jokes and a wicked imitation of Waymann saying 'I'd like a little word!'.

'Cool!' Ryan had laughed until his sides hurt.

'Don't make me laugh, Liam. I've got a stitch!' Lola had pleaded when the visitor did his Waymann voice again in front of Bex and Sasha. Sasha had jumped a mile, thinking it was the real thing.

'Look at what?' Wayne asked now, his hands covered in PVA glue from the cardboard dice he was making in class.

'This!' Tom cried, opening a matchbox and showing Wayne a severed finger.

'Yuck!' Wayne sprang back from the bloody object. 'It's still moving. Ergh, gross!'

Tom grinned and shoved the box under his nose a second time.

'It's fake, stupid!' Bex pushed Wayne aside to explain how Tom had cut a hole in the matchbox, lined it with cotton wool

covered in red paint, then stuck his finger
through. 'It's still attached to Tom's hand.
Wimp! Fancy falling for that old trick!'

A red-faced Wayne scraped himself off
the floor.

'It was my idea!' Liam boasted.

'Scary!' Ryan admitted, taking a closer
look.

'Not so scary as this!' Liam held up

a home-made spider shaped from pipe cleaners and hanging by an invisible thread. 'Whoo-oooh!'

He swung the furry scuttler in front of Bex, who squealed.

'Hah!' Tom gave a satisfied cry.

'Get lost, Tom Bean!' Bex lost her cool. 'Honestly, it's time you and your stupid cousin grew up!'

'Yeah, like you!' Tom retorted. He and Liam strolled away arm in arm chortling with laughter.

'Always act innocent!' was Liam's advice to Tom on the bus home. 'Never look as if anything is your fault. That's the way to work it.'

'What if you're caught red-handed?' Tom wanted to know. 'Like, you're in the park and you've crashed into an old woman on your skateboard and everyone's seen it was you.'

'Say you couldn't see because of your

hay fever,' Liam shot back. 'Or else you were rushing to save your deaf dog from being run over by a dustbin lorry!'

Tom nodded. 'Gotcha.'

'The crazier the better,' Liam advised. 'And always make your eyes really big, like this.' Liam flashed Tom a who-me? look.

'C'mon, this is our stop!' Leaving it almost too late, Tom led Liam down the stairs and hopped off the bus on to the pavement.

'Can you make a face like this?' Liam challenged, twisting his ears and sticking out his tongue. His eyes went squinty at the same time.

Tom copied him.
'Yeah, easy.'

'And like this?'
This time Liam blew
out his cheeks and
pushed his nose up
into a piggy snout.

'No prob!' Oink-oink!
Tom did a mega pig

impression, watching his reflection in a butcher's shop window.

'Beat it!' the butcher cried, waving a fat fist from inside the shop. 'Or I'll have your guts for garters!'

Tom and Liam laughed as they legged it.

'Hey, we nearly ended up as sausage meat!' Tom gasped.

'Yeah, Big Macs!' Liam stopped by the park to catch his breath. 'Listen, Tom, d'you want to learn a wicked trick?'

'You betcha!' By now, Tom was so impressed by Liam that he would have said yes to standing on his head on top of the Telecom Tower.

Liam and Tom jogged up the street and turned left down an alley into Tom's back garden.

'OK, now listen to this.' Liam stood face to face with Tom. 'You think of something to say.'

'Like what?' Tom was puzzled.

'Anything,' Liam insisted. 'Go on, say it.'

Tom cleared his throat. 'Let's go down the park with our skateboards.'

A split second later, Liam came back with the same words in Tom's exact same voice. 'Er-hum. Let's go down the park with our skateboards,' he said without moving his lips.

Startled, Tom looked round to see where the echo had come from.

'That was me!' Liam exclaimed. 'Say something else!'

Tom frowned. 'Witchy Waymann wobbles along,' he declared.

'Ichy Aymann obbles along,' Liam said. 'Hey, "w"s are mega hard,' he explained. 'And "b"s and "p"s. The rest of the alphabet is easy peasy.'

'Yeah, but how d'you make your voice sound like mine?' Tom wanted to know.

Liam shrugged. 'That's the tricky part. It's like those impressionists on TV. They listen really hard to what someone's saying, and how they're saying it, then, hey presto, they've got it!'

'Wow, cool!' Tom was eager to put Liam to the test. 'Come into the shed and listen to this,' he told him.

Leading the way, Tom entered the garden shed where his dad kept his budgies. There were thirty of the tiny, colourful birds swinging on swings, tweeting, chirping and fluttering from perch to perch.

Liam gave a low whistle. For once he had nothing to say.

'Like 'em?' Tom asked.

'Ye-ah,' Liam answered nervously as a green bird landed on his shoulder. 'Are they tame?' he asked.

Tom nodded. 'This one can talk,' he boasted, putting his finger out for Chippie to land on. Soon the blue and white budgie flew down from his perch. 'Listen!'

Chippie seemed to know he was on show. He cocked his head sideways and fixed his beady black eye on Liam. 'Chippie!' he squawked. 'Who's a cheeky boy?

Where's Thomas? Chip-chip-chippety-chip!'

It was Liam's turn to be impressed. 'Cool!' he whispered.

'Can you do Chippie's voice?'

Liam nodded. 'Chippie. Who's a cheeky boy?'

'Wicked!' Tom grinned, while Chippie squawked in annoyance and hopped back on to his perch.

Hey, dude, who's the joker?

'Does he say anything else?' Liam wanted to know.

'Not out loud,' Tom answered. He wasn't ready to tell Liam that he and the bird had deep and meaningful private conversations.

Man, he looks like trouble to me. Chippie's opinion of Liam was crystal clear. *You need to watch your back when he's around, dude!*

'The thing is, we could make out that Chippie can talk and say anything he wants,' Tom said. 'I'd have him on my shoulder and he would look as if he was answering, but really it would be you standing there doing your ventril-ventro-ventro-li-lo-kissed stuff!'

'Ventriloquist,' Liam corrected. He thought about Tom's plan. 'Like, who would we trick?' he asked.

'Mum, Dad, Nick–anyone who comes in the shed!' Tom couldn't wait to see the looks on his family's faces when Chippie talked about the weather, or the latest football results! 'What d'you think?' he pressed. 'Shall we give it a try?'

Slowly the doubtful frown eased from Liam's forehead. He'd quickly got used to the fluttery, pecking, hopping, cheep-cheepy pets, and he saw the funny side of what Tom was suggesting.

'Yo, dude!' he replied with a broad grin. 'You know me–I'll do anything for a laugh!'

Three

'What did one angel say to the other angel?' Liam whispered to Tom as they watched Harry Bean approach the shed.

'I dunno. What did one angel say to the other angel?' Tom was trying to tempt Chippie down from his perch with a tasty piece of cuttlefish.

'Halo!' Liam quipped. 'Get it? Halo-Hello!'

'Quiet a sec, I'm concentrating.'

Tom's dad had stopped outside the door to breathe in the warm evening air. He looked happy and relaxed after a day delivering mail, ready to enjoy his favourite pastime of looking after his feathered companions.

Tom made tweeting noises by puckering his lips. 'Here, Chippie, here, Chip!'

The budgie was not in a good mood. He ducked his head and spat out husks of birdseed. *Like, who is this Liam character? Get him outta my hair, will ya!*

'Quick, your dad's coming in!' Liam warned, turning to face the door and putting on a bright smile. 'Hi there, Uncle Harry. You've got some cool budgies in here.'

'Thank you, Liam. Did Tom tell you that every one of them has a name? This green one's Midge and this white one's called Snowflake. They all have different markings on their wing and tail feathers, so no two birds are exactly alike.'

'You don't say!' Liam kept Harry talking while Tom tempted Chippie on to his shoulder.

OK, OK, I'll nibble your cuttlefish. But don't expect me to suck up to the new kid. I don't like the guy and that's a fact.

'Chip-Chip-Chippie!' Tom murmured, tweeting and tutting as the bird landed with a flutter and a sharp dig with his claws. Ouch!

Yeah? Chippie eyeballed Tom.

'This one talks, doesn't he?' Liam asked Harry, pointing to Chippie.

'Yeah, a little bit,' Harry replied. 'Tom taught him to say a few words.'

'More than a few words!' Liam insisted. 'This budgie's dead clever. Listen to this!'

With a good-natured shrug, Harry paid attention.

'Ask Chippie a question,' Liam ordered Tom.

'OK. Chip, what d'you think of

the cuttlefish?' Tom asked.

'Yummy scrummy!' came the answer, loud, squawky and clear.

Harry's eyebrows shot up.

'Again!' Liam insisted.

Tom turned his head sideways and entered into deep conversation with the bird. 'Chippie, who d'you think will win the Premiership next season?'

Chippie tilted his head from side to side as if in deep thought. 'If United hang on to that Brazilian striker, it'll be their year. But if Steelers buy the German goalkeeper, and United lose their guy to the Italian team, it'll be us!'

'Strike a light!' Harry gasped, looking all around the shed.

'Chip-chip-chippety-chip!' Chippie squawked. *Dude, I'm serious. You gotta get rid of this kid!*

Tom grinned at his dad. 'I taught Chips some extra stuff,' he mumbled modestly.

Liam gave a secret wink. 'This budgie

is a genius. He's the Einstein of cage birds—
a superbrain!' Liam laid it on thick for a
flabbergasted Harry. 'Listen again.'

'OK, Chippie.' Tom had watched his dad's
jaw drop and was struggling to keep a
straight face. 'What's Mum making for
tea tonight?'

'Saghetti ologese.'

'Spaghett bolognese?'

'Yeah, man. Saghetti ologese.'

Harry frowned and went up close to
Chippie. He studied him from every angle.

Choking back a guffaw, Tom carried on
his conversation with Superbird. 'Why was
the sea wet?' he asked.

'I don't know. 'Hy as the sea et?'

Chippie squeaked.

Liam rolled his eyes at Tom. *Remember the 'w's!* Tom chuckled. 'Because the seaweed!'

'Wait–stop–hold on a second while I fetch your mum!' Harry stammered. He dashed to the door of the shed and yelled for Beth to come.

P-p-p-huh! Tom spluttered.

Chippie gave Tom's ear a hard peck.

'Sshhh!' Liam whispered. The ventriloquist trick had worked like a dream so far. He'd even been able to throw his voice so that it sounded like the words had been coming straight out of Chippie's sharp little beak.

'What's wrong?' Beth ran across the lawn, expecting a disaster. She came into the shed and closed the door behind her.

'What are you up to?' she demanded after one look at Tom's face.

'Listen, love. Either I'm hearing things, or we've got ourselves a bird in a million!' Harry said in a high, excited voice. 'Go on, Tom, make Chippie do it again.'

Tom coughed and spluttered. His face was red with the effort of trying not to laugh.

Liam stood to one side, looking as if butter wouldn't melt.

'Chippie, why did the sea blush?' Tom tried to ask. 'Chippie, why (splutter) did (snort) the sea (guffaw) blush (rip-snorting belly laugh)?'

'I dunno,' Chippie squawked. 'Hy did the sea lush?'

'Because it saw the ship's bottom!'

For a split second, Beth was taken in. She gasped in shock, then pulled herself up short. 'Tom, what's so funny?' she demanded.

By now Tom was laughing so hard that

he shook Chippie off his shoulder.
He clutched his stomach and spluttered
over Liam.

'Liam, why is Tom laughing?' Beth noted
the look of innocence on the face of her
nephew. She glanced from one to the other,
then at Chippie flying up to his perch.
A small light dawned inside her head. 'For
heaven's sake!' she said to Harry, hands
on her hips. 'Did you drag me all the way
over here to listen to Liam and Tom playing
one of their silly tricks?'

'Mum's not easy to fool,' Tom told Liam
when they lay in bed in Tom's room later
that night.

'Yeah, but if you'd kept a straight face, it
could've worked like it did with your dad,'
Liam insisted.

Tom rested with his hands behind his
head, looking back on an evening of jokes,
tricks, skateboarding in the park, then more
tricks. 'Get lost, Liam!' Nick had finally said

to his cousin after Liam had hidden the TV
remote behind a cushion for the third time.

'That's not very nice!' Tom had cried.

'Get lost, Tom,' Nick had insisted.

'I'd keep a straight face if you didn't wink
at me like crazy,' Tom said now. He felt that
Liam's visit was living up to expectations;
the two of them were managing to get up
everyone's noses big style.

'Wasn't that a great crack-your dad
thinking that Chippie must've swallowed a
whole dictionary!' Liam laughed.

'Yeah, and there's Mum saying not to
encourage me,' Tom recalled. 'She said she
has enough trouble keeping me under
control without you giving me lessons in
how to play practical jokes.'

'Wicked!' Liam chuckled. 'I like Auntie
Beth.'

Tom rolled over in bed. He was about to
sink into a cosy sleep when a brilliant idea
suddenly struck him. He sat straight up.
'Liam, y'know Nick?' he began.

'Yeah, course.' Liam too was drifting off into dreamland.

'D'you wanna play a mega trick on him tomorrow?'

'Yeah, sounds cool.' Zzzzz...

'I mean a really monster joke that even you wouldn't have thought of?' Tom buzzed with excitement. Wow, was he totally wicked, or what!

'Yeah, tell me tomorrow,' Liam mumbled sleepily.

'No, it won't wait. We have to make plans, use the computer after everyone's gone to bed. Wake up, Liam, this is what we're gonna do...!'

Four

'Sshh!' Tom warned Liam.

It was past midnight, the whole house was dark and silent as they crept downstairs in their PJs.

'I'm hungry!' Liam hissed.

Tom tutted. 'This is no time to think about your stomach!'

'Yeah, but I'm famished!' Liam snuck off into the kitchen and grabbed a handful of crunchy nut cornflakes from the box in the cupboard. Munch-munch-munch! He followed Tom into the TV room.

'Sshh!' Tom frowned. The TV room was under his mum and dad's bedroom. 'If they wake up, the whole plan will be wrecked!'

Crunching and munching, Liam watched Tom switch on the PC in the corner. 'You're sure this is gonna work?' he mumbled.

'Ssshhh! Yeah.'

Tom cringed as the computer hummed, beeped and burbled into action. 'Sshh!!' he told it. Then he chose a design program and began work.

Munch-swallow-gulp. Liam polished off the cornflake mush.
'Mmm, yummy!'

Parradise Pop Festival
Saterday and Sunday
4th & 5th July

Tom typed the words on the keyboard. The clickety-click of the keys seemed to echo all round the house.

'There's only one 'r' in Paradise,' Liam informed him.

'Smartarse!' Tom deleted the letter and continued.

Fun in the Sun
with
Mirage, TelX, Aimee,
Supersticious Minds
Andrew White
&
Big Sister

Typing with two fingers, he fumbled over the keys.

'Get a move on,' Liam yawned, wandering away to turn on the TV.

A blast of action movie music made Tom swivel round. 'Turn the volume down!' he yelped. Any minute now his mum would be thundering downstairs, wanting to know what the heck was going on.

Liam pressed the button. 'I don't know about this fake ticket thing,' he grumbled, flopping on to the sofa and watching a

PARADISE POP FESTIVAL
SATERDAY AND SUNDAY
4TH & 5TH JULY

Fun in the sun
with
Mirage, TelX, Aimee,
Supersticious Minds
Andrew White
&
BIG SISTER

£45 admit one

silent Bruce Willis smash through a window fifty floors up a tower block. 'Is it gonna be good enough to fool Nick?'

'Is Robbie Exley the best striker in the world?' Tom retorted, his face glowing blue in the light of the PC screen. The machine hummed loudly as he completed the design. 'Is the world round? Is...'

'Yeah, gotcha,' Liam sighed. Bruce had

just landed safely on the roof of a soft-top Cadillac. 'And you're telling me that Nick goes ga-ga over Big Sister?'

'Big time ga-ga,' Tom assured him, crouched over the keyboard, getting everything centred and choosing a wicked font. 'He fancies Serena. I reckon he'd kill to be able to see them live in concert.'

Adding a bit of clip art to make the whole ticket look cool and genuine, he finished off with:

£45

Admit one

'OK?' he checked with Liam, who gave the screen a quick glance and nodded. By now, Bruce was jumping through flames and rolling along the basement floor of a multi-storey car park, chased by five masked men with guns.

So Tom printed the ticket and trimmed it with scissors.

'Cool!' he decided. He stood in front of Liam and held the forgery up for inspection.

'Now you've gotta do your bit,' he reminded him in a dramatic whisper. 'If this trick's gonna work, the rest is up to you!'

'Did I hear you two get up in the middle of the night last night?' Beth asked at breakfast time.

Tom winced then nodded. 'Liam was famished,' he confessed. 'So we snuck down for something to eat.'

His mum plonked down the boxes of breakfast cereal, noting that the crunchy nut cornflakes packet was seriously lighter than it had been the day before. 'Boys!' she tutted. 'You have stomachs like huge, bottomless pits!'

Tom grunted vaguely while Liam dug into a giant bowl of Rice Crispies, washed down by apple juice.

'Why should I be surprised?' Beth wondered out loud. 'After all, I've had four sons and each of you could eat for England!'

Phew! Tom snuck a glance at Liam. He kicked him under the table as he heard Nick's bedroom door open. 'You got the ticket?' he hissed.

Liam produced the crumpled slip of paper from his pocket.

'Pity I can't use this myself!' he sighed, straightening it out and laying it flat on the table.

'What's that, Liam?' Beth asked, taking a kindly interest.

'It's a ticket for the Paradise Pop Festival,' he explained sadly as Nick slouched into the kitchen.

'Move over, you!' Shoving Tom along the bench at the table, Nick sat down, bleary-eyed. He reached for a bowl and a box of cereal.

'Aren't they like gold dust?' Beth inquired. 'Nick, weren't you trying to buy a Festival ticket for this weekend?'

'Huh?' Apeman replied.

'I said, weren't you desperate to get to

see that girl band you rave on about, but the tickets were all sold out?'

'Uh-huh,' Nick agreed.

Tom grinned to himself; so far so good!

'Well, would you believe it!' Liam said in a mega-stunned voice.

Watch it! Tom said to himself, afraid that his cousin was laying it on too thick.

'Huh?' Nick inquired.

'I said, would you believe it? It just so happens that we were talking about the gig and I *just so* happen to have a ticket myself right here!' Liam waved the white slip at Nick, his eyes shining brightly, a look of total amazement on his cheeky little face underneath his thatch of spiky hair.

'Isn't that a mega coincidence!'

Slowly Nick's eyes focused on the forgery. 'Are you going to the Festival?' he asked.

Like a fish swimming up to the maggot on the hook, ready to bite. Tom grinned to himself.

'I was going,' Liam reported. 'I was

planning to meet my older brother, Philip
and his girlfriend, Lynn. They were gonna
take me, we were gonna camp and
everything.'

'But?' Nick asked, a flicker of alertness
appearing in his eyes.

Liam sighed. 'But now Lynn's sister's had
a baby-it came really early. Lynn and Philip
aren't going any more-they're going to see
the baby instead. What a pain.'

Wow! Tom was speechless with
admiration.

'Hmm.' Nick pawed at the ticket on the
table. 'So this is going spare?'

Liam hung his head and nodded.

Tom watched his brother pick up the fake
with trembling fingers. 'How much d'you
want for it?' Nick grunted.

'Fifty pounds!' Liam shot back, his face
deadly serious. 'If you have the cash,
it's yours!'

'I thought you were gonna give us away!'

Liam told Tom as they stood at the bus stop and watched Nick cycle off down the road to school.

'I know. I could hardly keep my face straight,' Tom confessed. 'Nick looked like a goldfish!'

'Yeah-mouth open, stary eyes!' Liam enjoyed the memory. The two boys climbed on the bus, which passed Nick at the top of the hill. They pulled silly faces which Nick ignored.

'Mind you, I don't think you should've handed the ticket over until Nick had coughed up the dosh,' Tom pointed out.

He'd tried to stop Liam when Nick insisted on pocketing the forgery, but Liam hadn't seemed to mind that much about the fifty quid. 'The joke is that he believed us!' he'd explained later.

'He wanted to take it into school with him to show all his mates,' Liam recalled as the bus trundled downhill towards Woodbridge Juniors. By this time, Nick had

split off from the main road and was
cycling energetically towards his secondary
school on the other side of town.

'Yeah, wicked!' Tom pictured his brother
showing off. Nah-nah, I've got a ticket to
see Big Sister, and you haven't! Just like a
little kid. What a joke! 'Think about it–he'll
get to the gate of Paradise Fields on
Saturday morning, and the guy taking the
tickets will look at Nick's piece of paper
and tell him to get lost!'

Liam doubled up laughing.

'Look at those two silly idiots!' Bex
sniffed snootily from her seat at the back
of the bus.

Danielle and Sasha tutted.

'This is our stop!' Tom cried, leaping from
his seat and lurching down the aisle. He
and Liam clattered off the bus ready to lay
a trail of chaos through Registration,
Assembly, Numeracy and Science.

At dinner time Liam spilt a glass of water
all over Wayne, and in afternoon break

Tom trapped Fat Lennox in a small store room where Bernie King kept the polishing machine. In Silent Reading Liam slipped a whoopee cushion on Leftie's chair, then blamed Ryan.

'A good day!' Tom sighed happily as he and Liam headed for the door at half-past three.

'Mmmmm-m-m-mmmmm!' Lennox

whined from the store room.

'Oops!' Tom suddenly remembered what he'd done to Bernie's dog. He nipped back to open the door.

Lennox stumbled out, tripped and rolled. Groggily he picked himself up and waddled away.

'Tom Bean!' Mrs Waymann bellowed from fifty metres away. The headteacher had sharp eyes. She stormed down the corridor, ready to accuse Tom. 'I saw that! What did you do to that poor dog? How long has he been in there? I know for a fact that Mr King has been searching for Lennox all afternoon!'

'Please, miss, I just heard him whining!' Tom protested. 'I didn't do nothing!'

'You didn't do ANYthing!' Waymann corrected.

'Yes, miss. That's right, miss. I didn't do anything!' Tom's eyes were clear and bright as he stared straight back at the Head. 'I heard this noise of whining and scrabbling, so I opened the door and out pops Lennox!'

'Hmm.' Nine times out of ten, Mrs Waymann would have hauled Tom off to her office for a little word. But there was a staff meeting, and then a parents' evening to organise. 'Very well, off you go,' she muttered moodily.

Tom and Liam sprinted off.

'Cool!' Liam's praise for Tom's injured-innocent act was genuine. 'You're a quick learner!'

'Thanks,' Tom mumbled.

'Get a move on, you two!' Leftie called from the secretary's office, 'or you'll miss the bus.'

'Sir, we're walking home, sir!' Tom answered.

The young teacher strolled out of the office carrying his motorbike helmet. 'So, Liam, how are you enjoying your time with us?'

'It's rad, sir!'

Leftie pretended to be puzzled. 'Rad. Is that a good or a bad thing?'

'Rad, sir – radical. Y'know, mega, wicked, cool!' Tom helped him out.

'Oh, good.' Leftie smiled and walked with them out into the playground, towards the bike shed where his purple and black Yamaha was parked. 'How long have you got before you go home to Dublin?' he asked Liam.

'Just one more day, sir.' Then the cheeky visitor took a risk. 'Why–d'you wanna get rid of me?'

Leftie smiled. 'Don't push your luck, young Liam! And don't mention the word, "whoopee-cushion" to me either!'

'Me, sir?' Liam protested.

Leftie nodded. 'Yes, you, Liam. It was bit of a giveaway that the cushion was printed all over with a shamrock design, don't you think?'

Get out of that one! Tom thought. He was going to enjoy seeing Liam squirm for a change. But then a figure waiting at the gate caught his attention. It was half hidden by the iron railing and hedge,

but he could make out someone on a bike that looked suspiciously like Nick's yellow mountain bike.

'Er-hum!' he coughed.

'Sir, I gave the cushion to Ryan as a birthday present!' Liam told Leftie.

'Nice try, Liam. But Ryan's birthday happens to be in November.'

'Yes sir, it was an early birthday present!'

'Er-hum!' Tom coughed more loudly. That was definitely Nick at the gate, and he was obviously lying in wait for them. 'We gotta go!' he said hastily.

'That was very kind of you, Liam, and I'm sure Ryan appreciated it!' Leftie grinned. 'Well, I'll certainly miss you and your sense of humour after you've gone!'

'This way!' Tom grabbed Liam's arm and tried to pull him sideways behind the bike shed. But it was too late; Nick had already spotted them.

'Whoops!' Liam stepped back. 'What's Nick doing here?'

Tom saw the look on his brother's face. It was worse than a frown; more of a scowl, or even a hate-filled glare. In fact, it was the sort of look Bruce Willis got from the main man with the gun who was always trying to shoot him.

'I think he's gonna kill us!' Tom answered faintly.

Dumping his bike at the gate, Nick squared his shoulders and strode across the playground towards them.

Five

'You must think I'm stupid!' Nick yelled.

Liam and Tom looked aghast. *Who, us? No way!*

'This stupid ticket is a fake!' Nick roared.

More incredulous stares from Tom and Liam.

'This wouldn't fool anyone!'

Yeah, except you, birdbrain! Tom thought.

'What d'you mean, it's a fake?' Liam was

the first to put up a defence.

'I mean, it's a duff ticket–no good, useless, not worth the paper it's written on!' Nick glared from Liam to Tom. 'You made me look a right idiot in front of all my mates!'

'Whoah!' Liam backed off. 'Don't look at us. No way did we know it wasn't the real thing! I'd better get on the phone to Philip and warn him.'

But Nick wasn't listening. He waved the crumpled ticket in front of their faces. 'Look!' he yelled. 'They've spelt "Saturday" with an "e". And "admit" with two "d"s.'

Whoops! Tom swallowed hard. He should've run the spellcheck on it, since spelling had never been his thing.

Liam frowned, sneaking a sideways glance at Tom. 'Yeah, and look at Superstitious!'

'With a "c"!' Nick snorted furiously. 'So what happens when I show this stupid thing to Gaz and Ollie? I'm saying,

"Get a load of this. I'm on my way to Fun in the Sun, so feast your eyes, dummies!" Gaz grabs the ticket, gives it the once over and says, "You're the dummy, Nico! How much did you pay for this?"'

'Yeah, yeah, we gotcha!' Liam tried to stop Nick from bursting a blood vessel. 'I'll talk to my brother, he'll fix it, no problem.'

'Like, I believe that Philip gave you this ticket!' Nick yelled. 'Like, this isn't down to you, you sneaky little...!'

Nic in a mega-strop was not pretty. Tom watched his brother's face turn beetroot and practically saw the steam coming out of his ears.

'What were you doing downstairs last night?'

'Nothin'!'

'Scoffin' cornflakes!'

'You were on the computer!' Nick insisted. I heard you log on, so don't try to deny it!'

'Liam wanted to e-mail his dad.' Tom's limp excuse bit the dust.

'Don't give me that. I know what you were up to-forging this stupid ticket, that's what!'

By now, even Liam had run out of excuses.

'You rotten little, sneaky, cheating little...!' Nick advanced on Tom. 'I oughta beat you to a pulp, that's what!'

'Steady on, there!' Emerging from the bike shed wheeling his Yamaha, Leftie broke them up. 'What's the problem?'

Nick turned on the teacher. 'Ask them!' he yelled. 'These two just tried to cheat me out of fifty quid!'

'OK, calm down. Who are you and what exactly is going on?'

'I'm Tom's brother, and he's a cheating little rat!' Nick exploded. 'I used to come to this school!'

Leftie rolled his eyes and rested his bike on its stand. 'Oh no, not another member of the Bean clan!' he sighed. 'You must have been before my time.'

'Yeah, but Mr King will remember me,' Nick claimed. He'd spotted the caretaker and his dog stomping up out of the basement office. 'Hey, Mr King. It's me, Nick Bean!'

'Here comes trouble!' Bernie grunted.

Fat Lennox huffed and puffed his way across the tarmac. He avoided the group of angry people, waddled over to Nick's bike dumped at the gate, lifted his leg and had a wee. Then he clamped his jaws around the crossbar and began to drag the whole bike out on to the path.

'Hey, stop 'im!' Nick cried, as he saw his precious mountain bike being scragged about and scratched by the dumb bulldog.

'Leave it!' Bernie ordered Lennox.

The heavyweight bruiser ignored the command. Now the bike was in danger of being tossed like a piece of scrap metal on to the road.

'Hold it!' A frenzied Nick shot off across the playground to rescue his bike.

'Phew!' Tom heaved a sigh of relief. 'I hate to say it, but thank you, Lennox!'

Liam grinned. At least the heat was off them for the moment.

'That boy, Nick Bean, was every bit as bad as his younger brother,' Bernie grumbled to Leftie. 'Personally, I wouldn't trust 'im as far as I could throw 'im!'

'Your dog seems to be making a good job of throwing his bike out on to the busy road!' Leftie commented.

'Go, Lennox!' Tom whispered.

Tussle-tussle-scrape-shove! The Strongest

Dog in the World mangled Nick's machine.

'Look at it!' Nick yelled, grabbing the handlebars and tugging. It's scratched off the yellow paint!'

'Watch he dosn't sink his teeth into your tyres!' Liam warned. He and Leftie had run to help Nick, while Tom and Bernie took a back seat. Together they wrestled Fat Lennox for possession of the bike, and at last they won.

'I'm gonna make Bernie pay for repairs!' Nick complained. 'There's fifty quid's worth of damage here, easy! And I've got witnesses to prove it was his dog that did it!'

'Don't push your luck,' Leftie warned. Not having heard the full story, he had Nick down as an unruly teenager with a bad temper. 'We could just as easily say you were trespassing in the first place!'

Nick grunted. The young teacher, dressed in shiny black helmet and leathers, didn't look like someone to be messed with. So he turned to Tom. 'Don't think I've forgotten about the ticket!' he muttered. 'Just as soon as I've taken this bike to the repair shop, I'll come looking for you, don't you worry!'

Tom hid behind Leftie and Bernie, wishing that Liam would mind his own business and stop sucking up to Nick.

'Here's your bike,' Liam offered, too helpful by half. 'The saddle's only a bit scraped, and the handlbars aren't too bad.'

Nick wrenched the bike from him. 'And you!' he warned. 'Knowing you, you were in on this right from the start!'

Tom did what he had to do, stepping forward with a confession and speaking up for his cousin. 'No, he wasn't! It was only me – it was my idea, and I did the whole joke, honest!'

'Huh!' Nick laughed. 'You're talking about a kid that hasn't stopped playing tricks since he stepped inside our house!'

'Yeah, but this time it was just me!' Tom insisted.

Liam was looking at him and shaking his head. Bad idea. Never own up to anything, dude!

Laughing again, Nick straddled the scratched crossbar and perched on the high saddle. 'I'm not listening!' he retorted. 'I'm saying, watch out, both of you!'

'That's enough,' Leftie insisted. 'And Tom, don't worry. I'm going to go straight back into school and give your mum a ring to tell her what's been going on.'

Tom gasped. 'No sir, don't do that!'

'Yep. I've made up my mind. There's a family problem here, and it's my job to help to sort it out.'

Bernie nodded. 'Beth Bean will handle it,' he confirmed. 'She never takes any nonsense.'

'No, please, sir!' Tom hopped and jumped like a cat on hot bricks as Leftie went back inside.

Meanwhile, Liam was warning Nick about something urgent.

'Gerroff!' Nick growled.

'I'm not touching you!' Liam blocked the way, desperately trying to stop Nick from cycling off down the hill. 'Listen, don't go! Look–Lennox chewed through that cable. Now the brakes won't work!'

'Hah-hah, don't make me laugh!' Angrily Nick pushed Liam out of his way. 'You crack me up, you really do!'

'No, I'm serious!' Liam fell into the hedge and ate privet leaves. Yuck. Spit. 'You've got no brakes on that bike, Nick. If you don't believe me, take a look!'

'Get lost!' Nick told him.

He put one foot on one pedal and shoved off with the other.

'Don't do it!' Liam cried from the bottom of the hedge. 'I'm telling you the truth for once!'

Nick rode off the pavement into the traffic, swerving between two parked cars and joining in the flow of traffic. 'Tell Tom not to bother to hide, 'cos I'll find you!' he flung back over his shoulder.

'The brakes won't work!' Liam said faintly, watching in horror as Nick overtook a bus at a bus stop and sped on down the hill.

Six

'Nick can't stop! His brakes are busted!'
Liam burst into the school secretary's office
where Leftie was making the phone call to
Tom's mum.

'Yeah, yeah!' Tom sighed. Now was not
the time for one of Liam's little jokes.

'I'm serious!' Liam gasped. 'The dog
chewed the cable, but Nick wouldn't listen
to me. He's gonna crash any second now!'

Tom frowned. This was so unreal it might actually be true!

Leftie must have thought so too, because he slammed down the phone without getting through to Beth, grabbed his helmet and set off at a run. 'I'll take my bike!' he called to Tom and Liam. 'You two follow on foot!'

So they raced out of the school grounds, with the roar of Leftie's motorbike starting up in their ears. They sprinted downhill, swerving round old ladies and women with pushchairs, dreading the sight of Nick splatted on the road.

'Maybe he'll bail on to a grass verge,' Liam suggested.

'There aren't any,' Tom pointed out. There were only roads and pavements, pedestrian crossings and one set of traffic lights all the way down to the park.

'Watch it, you kids!' One of the old ladies hit back with her rolled up brolly.

'Ouch!' Liam got it on the shins.

'Have you seen a kid on a runaway bike?' Tom asked a traffic warden who was writing a ticket for a car parked half on the pavement.

'Yep,' she said without looking up. 'He was breaking every traffic regulation in the book.'

'That's my brother!' Tom gabbled. 'Fat Lennox chewed his brake cable. He's out of control. There's gonna be a major accident!'

The traffic warden carried on writing the ticket. 'There's gonna be a major arrest when I call the police,' she grunted. 'Now shove off!'

Thanks for nothing! Tom heard Leftie's motorbike heading full throttle down the hill. He watched their teacher nip in and out of the slow-moving cars and trucks, crouched low over the handlebars and revving like mad.

'And I got his number, too!' the traffic warden muttered, writing it down on the back of her pad.

'That's our teacher!' Tom protested.
'He's trying to save Nick's life. You can't
book him!'

'I said, shove off!' the warden insisted,
glaring fiercely at them from under the
peak of her shiny black and yellow hat.

So Tom and Liam scarpered. There was
still no sign of a splatted Nick, and by
now Leftie himself had got snarled up

in traffic brought to a halt at the green
man crossing.

'Maybe Nick made it OK!' Tom gasped,
almost bumping into the post with the
flashing orange ball. 'He's an ace rider.
He goes off on cross-country trails and
does wheelies and everything.'

Liam overtook Tom on a bend. 'Let's
ask this man in the ice-cream van!'

He screeched to a halt beside Mr Whippy. 'Did you see a kid on a bike?' he gabbled.

The man leaned out across his counter. 'Come again?'

'I said, did you see a kid on a runaway bike?'

'Now listen to that. If that isn't a lovely Liffey lilt, ye can call me an eejit!' Mr Whippy smiled softly. He was an old man with lots of white hair and a few missing teeth. 'Meself and me missus, we came over from the old place thirty years back, but there isn't a day goes by that I don't miss that Dublin accent!'

'Yeah, cool!' Liam began to wish that they hadn't stopped. 'The thing is, we're looking for a kid on a bike. Did you see him?'

The old man scratched his head. 'I've seen a hundred kids on a hundred bikes. Which one in particular would you be looking for?'

Tom tried to hurry things up with a quick

description of Nick. 'He's tall and skinny. He's got messy hair and freckles. He looks like an older version of me!'

'On a yellow bike!' Liam added.

Mr Whippy thought hard. 'Now would he be yelling for people to get out of his way?' he asked.

'Yes!' Liam and Tom chorused.

'And would he be asking for help?'

'Yes!'

'Saying something about not having any brakes?'

'Ye-es!' Tom and Liam almost screamed back.

'...Ah no, I didn't see him.'

Uh? The boys sagged with disappointment.

'But a nice girl called Rebecca who bought a 99 from me a little while back said she'd seen him speeding across the main road, in front of a bus, followed by a white bulldog...'

Tom and Liam groaned.

'The girl said it nearly caused an accident. A passenger jumped off the bus and gave chase, but the boy never stopped.

'That's 'cos he couldn't,' Tom pointed out. No one seemed to have grasped this important fact. 'His brakes are busted. Nick could get himself killed!'

'Well, Rebecca and her two little friends went off after him, along with the passenger from the bus,' Mr Whippy reassured them. 'To be sure, it'll turn out fine!'

Rebecca? Two little friends? Bex? Danielle and Sasha? That was all they needed! Tom and Liam gathered their breath and pounded on down the street.

'Watch it!' a cross mother with a pushchair yelled. The toddler waggled his fat limbs and wailed.

'Kids!' a man in a suit complained, as Liam and Tom ducked and dived towards the main road.

'Any clues?' Leftie called from his

motorbike, once the traffic jam had eased and he was able to pull up alongside the boys.

'Nick made it across the main road!' Tom reported. 'Lennox was chasing him. They must've reached the park by now!'

'Right, I'll see you down there,' Leftie promised, va-va-vrooming off on his Yamaha.

The boys did the leg work, stopping for the red man, then darting across the road, still dreading the sight of a mangled mountain bike, and the wah-wahing wail of an ambulance siren.

But they reached the park gates without seeing any signs of catastrophe. Maybe, just maybe, Nick was going to be OK after all.

But then, 'Oh jeez!' Liam cried.

'Bummer!' Tom groaned.

There before their eyes lay a scene of total chaos.

'Bloomin' Nora!' Liam sighed.

Tom turned, ready to run. 'I'm outta here!'

Liam grabbed him. 'Oh no you don't! Nick's in BIG trouble. Like, HUGE!'

'Yeah!' Tom agreed. 'That's why I'm leggin' it!

'Chicken!' Liam charged on. 'Wow, look at that! Oops! Wow! Watch out! Wicked!'

Tom looked on with half-closed eyes. OK, so Nick and his runaway bike had made it to the park in one piece, but that must have been when his problems had really begun.

For a start, there were tyre marks through the flowerbeds. Roses were uprooted, fuchsias were flattened.

Then there were the furious footballers yelling at Fat Lennox to bring back their ball.

Plus skateboarders swerving to avoid Bex, Danielle and Sasha, who were screaming at Nick to stop before he crashed into the bouncy castle.

Then there was Harry sprinting down the hill to cut Nick off.

('Dad!' Tom did a double-take. How did he get here?)

Worst of all, there was Nick, five seconds away from making a crash landing.

Whoosh! Nick zoomed across the grass. Swish! He swerved madly to avoid the giant yellow and red inflatable. Bonk! He hit the plastic wall.

Hisssssssss!

'Wicked!' Liam crowed.

Ssssssssssss! The bouncy castle shrivelled. Three bouncing kids sank to the ground.

'Nick, look what you've done!' Dob-'em-in Danielle blurted out.

Sasha hung back well out of the way. Bex stood with her hands on her hips, sensibly saying nothing.

Ssssss! The last gasp of air escaped from the castle as an angry man emerged from a nearby van.

'Crash landing, neeyah–smack! Ryan abandoned his skateboard, spread his wings and jetted over. 'Emergency!

82

Mayday, Mayday!'

'Rad!' Kingsley was enjoying the show. He too ditched his board and came to spectate.

'Huh–wh-wh-what happened?' Nick was dazed from the soft collision.

'You nearly got yourself killed, that's what happened.' Harry ran up and seized Nick's bike.

Fat Lennox, who had been barking, yapping, snarling, hrrruffing, huffing and puffing in circles, now hurled himself at the bike. He tussled with Harry while Nick picked himself up and dusted himself down.

'Tom, come and lend a hand!' Harry yelled. 'Grab the dog's collar, hold him back!'

Easier said than done. Tom launched himself at Lennox, who swerved out of the way. Splat! He landed in a heap of shrivelled plastic among three bawling kids.

Hrrrufff! Fat Lennox turned his slavering

chops on Tom, who rolled off the deflated castle, up against the feet of Mr Bouncy.

'What happened?' The man stared at his once lovely inflatable. He was big, round and red, as if someone had blown *him* full of air. His curly hair was the shade of carrots, his yellow T-shirt displayed the scarlet logo, 'Castles In The Air'. 'This lot is worth thousands of pounds,' he complained. 'And now some stupid kid on a bike goes and wrecks it!'

Harry managed to ignore the man for the time being. 'Are you OK, son?' he asked Nick. 'You haven't broken anything, have you?'

'I'm fine,' Nick replied. 'But that rotten Liam won't be when I get my hands on him!'

'You'll have to pay for the damage!' Angry Man insisted. 'My business is ruined if I don't get it repaired double quick. My next booking's tomorrow, so I need the cash up front!'

'Later,' Harry answered, still worried about Nick. He gave the man his phone number and set off with his shaky son and the beaten-up bike.

Hrrruhhh!! Lennox growled. The barrel-shaped dog decided it was time for him to exit. He started at a slow trundle up the hill towards the park gates.

'Ruined!' Mr Bouncy yelled. 'And I'm not insured against some stupid kid on a bike crashing into Sleeping Beauty's Castle!'

'Er-hum!'

Tom heard Liam cough. What was his cousin up to now?

'Er-hum!'

'Whad'ya want?' Mr Bouncy snarled.

'Mister, I was wonderin'–would the insurance people give you the money if it was a dog with sharp teeth that had ruined the bouncy castle?' Liam gazed up at the owner with his wide, clear eyes.

'A dog?' Mr Angry echoed.

'Yeah. A big one with teeth like this.' Liam

gnashed his own teeth. 'They'd go straight through the plastic and rip it to shreds!'

The man frowned. 'Sure they would,' he grunted. 'Why?'

This was when Liam took a deep breath and timed his answer just right. Because that's exactly what happened!' he announced, taking the owner around the far side of the collapsed inflatable. 'That white dog sank his fangs in right here, where this rip is.'

'Phuh!' The man blew out his cheeks in surprise.

Liam spread his hands and came over deadly serious. 'Don't blame the kid on the bike. It was the dog that did it. Gnash-hisssss! Honest-I saw it with my very own eyes!'

Seven

'Ace!' Tom told Liam as they trotted
home. 'Quick thinkin'–that was the best lie
I ever heard.'

'That was no lie!' Liam protested.
'That was the whole truth and nothing but
the truth!'

'The hole truth!' Tom laughed. 'Whole-
hole–get it?'

They were laughing and joking as they

made their way up Tom's street.

'Did you see carrot-top's face when you said it was Lennox?' Tom exploded. 'I thought he was gonna rise up in the air like a helium balloon!'

'Yeah, but we managed to convince him,' Liam remembered. 'And we told 'im we'd never seen the dog before, that it must be some stray out on the loose.'

'Yeah, so now no one gets it in the neck, not even Lennox. And the man gets the money from his insurance!' Whether or not it was true about Bernie's dog ripping the hole in the castle, Tom still thought Liam was brill. 'Nick's off the hook and he's gonna have to be grateful to us big time!'

'Guilty, m'lud!' Liam grinned as he pictured Fat Lennox putting in his plea to the judge at his trial. 'It's a fair cop. It was me what punctured the yellow bouncy thingy wiv me gnashers!'

Tom shook with laughter as they went into the house. He felt prouder than ever to be Liam's cousin; with Kingsley, Ryan, Lola, Bex, Danielle and the rest looking on, Liam had pulled off a major victory over an angry grown-up. This would be guaranteed to make him the main man at school tomorrow–Liam's last day before Tom's aunt arrived to cart her son off back to Dublin.

'What d'you get if you cross a kangaroo with a sheep?' Liam asked.

Tom knew the answer but he played the game anyway. 'I dunno. What d'you get if you cross a kangaroo with...'

'Here he is!' Nick flew out of the kitchen into the hallway. 'I'll kill 'im if I get my hands on 'im!'

Nick was like a whirlwind sweeping Liam off his feet. Within a split second, he had his young cousin backed against the wall, throttling him with both hands before Tom could leap on to his brother from behind, cling like a monkey and drag him back.

'Hang on!' he cried. 'Liam just saved your bacon, if you did but know it!'

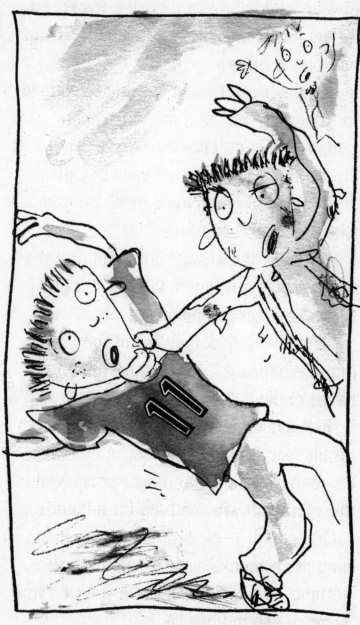

Nick staggered back, then threw Tom aside. 'You must be joking!' he cried. 'This little rat needs to be taught a lesson and I'm gonna do it right this minute with my own bare hands!'

'Lay off!' Tom leapt a second time. 'Liam managed to blame Lennox for the whole thing. Hey, are you listening, you cloth-eared baboon?'

Ignoring Tom's insults, Nick went at Liam like a mad thing. He pinned him up against the wall a second time. 'I'm not talking about that!' he yelled. 'I'm talking about the idiot thinking it was funny ha-ha to cut through my brake cable in the playground!'

Tom gaped. Liam turned pale. 'No way would I do that!' he gasped.

'Yeah, you did!' Nick had a crazy glint in his eye. 'You'd do anything for a laugh!'

'He wouldn't–he didn't!' Tom tried to wriggle between Nick and Liam. 'I was a witness. I was there, remember!'

'Yeah, and you would stick up for the

little skunk, wouldn't you! You're both as bad as one another!'

'OK, break it up!' Harry Bean ran in from the garden where Beth had stayed to talk to Mr Wright. He piled into the fight and separated the three boys. 'Your teacher's out there, Tom, trying to explain to your mother what's been going on. We've been through enough today without him seeing you three brawling like this!'

Gasping for breath, Tom stepped back. This was crazy. Nick was nuts. He saw it now; the sad fact was he belonged to a family of lunatics.

'Mr Wright took a detour from the park, once he saw that I'd jumped off the bus to help and that Nick hadn't been hurt,' Harry went on. 'He thought your mother deserved an explanation before we all got back.'

'Good!' Tom clung to the hope that Leftie would leap to Liam's defence. He ran outside, dragged his teacher into the house

and put it to him straight. 'Tell them that
Liam didn't cut Nick's cable!' he demanded.

'Tell them he did!' Nick cut in.

'Tell them it was Lennox!' Tom insisted.

Beth strode into the middle of it. 'Boys,
go to your rooms!' The main woman had
spoken. Tom whined and Nick grunted,
but they did as they were told and
slunk upstairs.

'I'm sorry, I can't really be of any help
over this cable business,' Leftie was saying.
'I didn't see that part.'

Tom shook his head. He turned to see
Liam still standing in the hallway, his face
white as a sheet. *Go on, think your way out
of it!* Tom begged silently. *Give them a
good story. Stick up for yourself like you
always do!*

But Liam was silent. No jokes, no excuses.
Only the shocked white face.

'Leave it until tomorrow,' Beth said,
apologising to Leftie and showing him to
the door. 'Liam's mum is due here in the

morning. I'll keep the boys off school so we can discuss it with her. One way or the other we'll see if we can't get to the bottom of this whole affair!'

Tom turned over in bed and sighed in his sleep. He turned again. In his dream an inflatable giant with carroty-red hair chased him through a dark forest. Tom was well ahead until a tree root twisted up like a black snake and wound itself round his ankle.

Splat! Tom fell full length and jerked awake.

Uh! What time was it? He opened one eye and saw that it was light. His alarm clock told him that it was 5.30am.

Uhhh! He pulled the duvet over his head and tried to go back to sleep.

Tweet-tweet, trill-trill. The birds in the trees set up their dawn chorus. Tom grew hot and poked his head out again. Stoopid birds cheep-cheeping away! He glanced across the room to find out if Liam was still asleep in the spare bed, then he sat bolt upright.

Liam's bed was empty.

Empty, as in 'no one there!'

Tom's stomach flipped. No, wait! Maybe Liam had gone for a pee. He forced himself to listen hard. Nope; no one was in the bathroom. OK then; Liam was downstairs chomping cereal. Listen again. Nothing, not a squeak.

Tom stared again at the empty bed. There was a note on the pillow. He leapt across the room and grabbed it:

Tom's heart jumped and missed a beat. 'Mum, Dad, come here quick!' he screeched. 'Liam's legged it!'

Harry appeared in his PJs. He was still at home because it was his day off from delivering the post. 'What's the panic?' he mumbled.

Tom thrust the note at him. 'Liam's run away. He left this.'

'Come off it.' Harry didn't believe a word. 'This is another of your practical jokes, isn't it?'

'No, Dad, honest!! I'm serious. Read the note. I just woke up and Liam was gone!!'

'Steady on,' Beth told him. She was tying her dressing-gown belt and stepping in to take control. 'Getting worked up won't help. Let me see the note. Hmm. Right, he can't have gone far. Let's start looking right away.'

Six o'clock and the birds were in full song. But Liam was still missing.

Six-thirty and the milkman delivered the milk. 'What are you lot doing up so early?' he asked.

'Mike, you haven't seen a young lad roaming the streets, have you?' Harry asked. By this time, Tom and his mum and dad were fully dressed. They'd searched the house from top to bottom.

'No. Why? Have you lost one?' the milkman inquired.

So Beth described Liam and Mike promised to keep an eye open. 'I'll send him home with a flea in his ear if I see him,' he promised.

Seven o'clock and Tom had run up and down the street asking everyone he met: 'Have you seen my cousin Liam? He looks like me with a baseball cap and a black T-shirt and baggies.'

'Is he lost?' the newspaper delivery girl quizzed.

'No, he ran away.'

'Tsk!' The girl raised her eyebrows.

'What did you do to him?'

'Nothin'! Oh never mind, forget it!' Tom ran on, looking behind every wheelie bin and under every hedge.

'Any sign?' Harry asked when Tom landed back home. Tom shook his head. 'He's vanished!' he gasped.

'Then maybe we'd better get in touch with the police to report him missing,' his dad said slowly.

Beth sighed. 'The only room we have't looked in is Nick's. I know he's still sleeping but d'you think we should...?'

'No!' Tom would've bet a million pounds that Liam wouldn't be there. 'Unless we're looking for a dead body!' he said darkly.

'Oh Tom, Nick's not that bad!' his mum protested. 'He wouldn't actually harm Liam, however angry he is.'

Tom glowered. 'You wanna bet?' She hadn't seen Nick trying to throttle poor Liam yesterday.

'Well, at least we should call your sister,'

Harry suggested. 'Will she have set off from London by now?'

Making calculations, Beth decided to contact Karen on her mobile. The others waited as she passed on the bad news.

'...Yes, before six this morning...there's a note...Yes, he'd got himself into a bit of bother with our Nick...I know you said he was a livewire, and he is, it's true. But to be honest, Karen, it was nothing we couldn't have sorted out between us.'

'It's all Nick's fault!' Tom muttered. 'He blamed Liam for the brakes, when really Liam saved Nick from the bouncy castle man and Nick didn't even believe us, and...'

'Pipe down, Tom,' Harry warned. 'Let your mum and auntie decide what to do.'

Typical! They never listened. Tom grabbed his skateboard and stormed off. He would actually do something to find Liam rather than standing around talking about it and wasting time. Looking at his watch, he saw that it was a quarter past seven.

I'll try the park, he decided, skating speedily to the gates. Liam knew this place and might have picked on it as his best hiding place. Tom ollied up the kerb and kickturned around corners. He pulled a 180 frontside slide to slow down by the kids' play area and take a look under the slide and behind the climbing frame. Nope; no Liam. So Tom skated on.

Where would I go if I was him? he asked himself, tic-tacking along the riverside path towards the old bridge. *Would I hide in the boatshed?*

Nope. A thorough search came up with the wrong result.

Or under the stone arches?

Tom hopped off his board and took a look under the bridge.

'Waaack-waaackk!' A mother duck shooed him away from her four cute ducklings.

Nope, Liam wasn't here either.

Super-sleuth Tom began to run out of ideas.

Maybe up a tree or hiding in the bushes? Phew, needle-in-a-haystack stuff! Tom skated into every corner of the park without any luck. Zero. Zilch. Big fat nothing!

So I was wrong, Tom told himself, heading for home with his fingers crossed that Liam had shown up of his own free will. After all, it was breakfast-time and hunger might drive him out into the open, especially if it was bacon sizzling in the pan and toast popping up warm and fresh out of the toaster...

But no; his dad came to greet him with an update–there was still no sign of the runaway, and Beth and Karen had decided that if Liam hadn't shown up by eight o'clock, then they would call the police.

Bummer! Tom's heart sank at the news that the police would soon be involved. *This is mega serious!* he told himself, stomping upstairs and hammering on Nick's door.

'I hope you're happy now!' he yelled. 'Liam's gone missing, all because of you!'

'Naff off!' came the reply.

Tom stomped down again and out to the shed. 'Bummer!' he told Chippie. 'Liam's legged it, and it's stoopid Nick's fault!'

Yo, dude, tell me about it! The budgie landed on Tom's head and tweaked his fringe.

'It's a long story,' Tom sighed. 'You don't wanna know.'

Try me, Chippie offered. *I'm all ears.*

'The whole thing's gone pear-shaped. For a start, stoopid Nick nearly kills himself on his bike, and he finally smashes into a bouncy castle.'

A what-castle, dude? The bird swung himself down on to Tom's ear and hung upside down from his lobe.

'A bouncy castle, for kids to bounce on. Everyone knows what they are.

Not me, man. I never heard of castles that bounce.

'No, the castles don't bounce,' Tom sighed. 'Never mind. The thing is, Chip,

I'm dead worried about Liam. He legged it and now thy're gonna call the police.'

No way! The budgie swung himself upright and trotted up on to the top of Tom's head. *Are you sure they checked the joint thoroughly?*

'We looked everywhere,' Tom told him. 'I just went down the park to see if Liam had hidden down there.'

Chippie fluttered from Tom's head on to a nearby perch so he could look him in the eye. *So now they panic and call the cops!* he declared.

'What else can they do?' At his wits' end, Tom paced up and down the small shed, scattering birds as he walked. Flutter–squawk-hop-skip-flutter.

Think again! Chippie insisted. He hopped up and down, bobbed his speckled head and scuttled along his perch. *You have a few million brain cells, don't you, dude?*

'Think again?' Tom said, frowning deeply. What was the bird on about? What did

Chippie know that no one else knew?

Where could this Liam kid be? Chippie demanded. *If he ain't in the house, and he ain't in the street, and he ain't in the park, where's he gonna hide, for chrissakes!*

Eight

'I am thinking!' Tom insisted.

Not hard enough. Chippie took off from his perch and flew around the shed. He landed near the small window. *Man, you can see the whole world from here!*

Tom joined him at the window.

Here come the cops! Chippie warned.

Sure enough, a white car with an orange stripe drew up at the garden gate.

A woman in a uniform came up the path.

'Bummer!' Tom groaned, turning restlessly away.

Quit talking like that. Chippie ducked his head crossly. *Didn't you hear what I said: you can see everything that goes off from this window.*

Tom stopped in his tracks. He crept back to Chippie's lookout point. Yeah; you could see the garden, the house, the door opening for Tom's mum to let the police officer in...

'Hey!' he cried.

Hay is what horses eat, Chippie pointed out.

Tom turned to him. 'Did you see what happened to Liam?' he demanded.

There was a silence as the bird cocked his head to one side.

'Did you?'

Maybe.

'No, really! Did you?'

'Who's a cheeky boy?' Chippie chattered.

'Chip-chip-chippety-chip! Who's a cheeky boy!'

'Don't give me that–you saw Liam leg it!' Tom accused. His heart raced, his mouth was dry as he advanced on the bird.

Chippie hopped nervously out of reach. *OK, you'd better come out and give yourself up, dude!* he told the person hiding in the birdseed cupboard. *I ain't gonna risk my neck to save your skin–no way!*

'In my birdseed cupboard!' Harry was lost for words.

'Yeah, I found him,' Tom boasted.

'No, you never. I gave myself up!' Liam claimed.

Beth had apologised to the police officer and seen her on her way after Liam had said sorry for all the trouble he'd caused. 'I only wanted to run away for a bit,' he explained. 'So Mam wouldn't kill me when she got here.'

Harry Bean shook his head. 'I'm not sure

I get the logic of that,' he muttered. 'Surely she'd kill you anyway when you eventually turned up.'

'Never mind now, Harry.' Beth put bacon and eggs in front of two starving boys. 'I'm sure Liam knows what he means.'

'I know I'm starving hungry!' Liam sighed, tucking in with gusto.

'Pass the ketchup,' Tom demanded, mid-chomp.

'Y'know what–Tom talks to the birds!' Liam dobbed his cousin in big time. 'He thinks they can talk back!'

'Don't!'

'Do!'

'Don't!!'

'Do!! I heard you!!'

'So what!' Tom didn't care any more. He'd been the one who discovered where Liam was hiding, and that was all that mattered.

Chomp-chomp-swallow. The tomato ketchup made the bacon slide down a treat.

'What did Mam say when you rang

her, Auntie Beth?' Liam paused mid-bite
to think ahead.

'She said, "That's it, that's Liam down to
a T, giving everyone a good scare with one
of his jokes!"' Beth repeated the message
word for word.

'I wasn't joking!' Liam protested. 'I really
really meant it.'

'And we weren't laughing for once,' Harry

told him. 'In future, I don't recommend
running away as a long-term solution to
your problems.'

Liam nodded and tucked in again, trying
to ignore the heavy footsteps on the stairs.

'It's the Abominable Snowman!' Tom
hissed. 'No, it isn't, it's the Monster from
the Deep!'

'Good morning, Nick,' Beth said breezily. 'I

see you slept through all the excitement for a change!'

Nick slumped down at the table, opposite Liam. 'I've been thinking...' he mumbled.

'Ouch!' Tom mocked. 'Careful you don't strain yourself!'

Nick flicked a cornflake at him without looking. 'I think maybe I went a bit over the top yesterday,' he told Liam. 'I mean, it was probably out of order to blame you about those brakes.'

Liam and Tom stopped chewing.

'Close your mouth when you've got food in it, Tom,' Beth reminded him.

'Thinking about it...' Nick went on.

'Ouch! Ooch! Don't–it hurts!'

'Shurrup Tom!' Nick snapped, then went on doggedly. 'Thinking about it, it must have been Lennox,' he admitted to Liam, 'because you didn't have anything sharp to cut that cable with.'

Liam gulped and nodded.

'Is that an apology I hear?' Beth wanted to know.

Nick frowned. 'Yeah,' he grunted.

'Well?'

'Well what?'

'I'm waiting for one little word beginning with "s".'

'S-s-sorry, Liam,' Nick stammered. 'It was only because you'd been such a pain in the neck that I thought it must be you.'

'Wicked!' Tom slapped Liam on the back. It was 8.45am. They were out of trouble and on their way to school.

'You want to go to school!' Beth had pretended to fall over with shock. 'Are you sure you don't want to take the day off?'

Liam and Tom had nodded.

'We want to go and see Kingsley and the gang,' Tom had explained. 'When we tell them what happened, they're never gonna believe us!'

'Let me get this straight: Tom Bean *wants* to go to school!' His mum had sat down with a strong cup of coffee.

Tom had even agreed to have a quick shower and get himself wet almost all over.

Now they were approaching the school gates, he and Liam arm in arm.

'The thing is, Mam will arrive at your house and your mam will have time to calm her down before we get back.' Liam was explaining to Tom his reason for volunteering for a day in class.

'Good thinking!' Tom approved.

'Hey Tom! Hey Liam!' Kingsley ran out to greet them. He gathered the rest of the gang, who came crowding round.

'Neeyah-boom-boom-neeyah! Tell us a joke, Liam!' Ryan demanded.

Liam beamed at them all. 'Shall I?' he asked Tom.

Tom grinned and nodded. It had been mega having his cousin to stay.

'Yeah!' he told him, ready to laugh and splutter all the way past Fat Lennox in his basement and Waymann in her office.

'OK, what goes "ha-ha-ha-clonk"?' Liam asked.

'We don't know. What goes "ha-ha-ha-clonk"?' everyone chorused.

'A man laughing his head off!' Liam replied.

'Ergh, that's gross!' Danielle wailed.

'I've heard it before!' Kingsley yelled.

'OK,' Liam went on, leading the way between the main doors. 'What goes

"mooz-mooz"?'

'Two cows?' Wayne guessed.

Tom followed close on Liam's heels.
He knew the answer and niftily stole the
punchline from his joker cousin. 'A plane
flying backwards!' he cried.

Boo-boom! Ha-ha! Wicked!

Look out for more
Totally Tom adventures!

Tell Me the Truth, Tom!

Jenny Oldfield

Tom eyeballs a fox in Bernie King's
basement, but no one believes him.
'No way! Dream on, Tom!' say his friends.
Tom decides to prove it. He's going to take
a picture of the fox... After all, the camera
never lies... Does it?

Watch Out, Wayne

Jenny Oldfield

Life's tough for Tom. He offers to be best
mates with new boy, Wayne, but it only lands
him in trouble – again! OK, maybe giving
Wayne a CRASH course in skateboarding
wasn't so smart.
But Tom meant well. Honest!

Get Lost, Lola

Jenny Oldfield

Tom is TOTALLY disgusted. Lola – aka, Little
Miss Superglue – says she fancies him. Ergh!
And Lola knows a shameful secret about Tom.
If he doesn't agree to be her boyfriend,
then the whole school will know it, too... Uh-oh!
But would Lola really be that devious
and mean?

Keep the Noise Down, Kingsley

Jenny Oldfield

Tom has a rival at school. Kingsley is a
mega-annoying show-off! He's lairy, he's
brash, and he's really getting on everyone's
nerves! Tom needs to find a way to break
it to Kingsley that he's got to pipe down!
But how?

Drop Dead, Danielle

Jenny Oldfield

Mean and mardy 'dob-'em-in' Danielle is on
Tom's case again–accusing him of flooding
the school cloakroom! *As if.* Danielle says
she's going to tell on Tom–and she probably
will! Tom needs to prove it wasn't
him–but how?

Look out for the adventures of Tom's sparky schoolfriend-Definitely Daisy!

Just You Wait, Winona!

Jenny Oldfield

Winona's a goody goody who sticks like glue and threatens to ruin Daisy's street cred. Daisy can't deal with a teacher's pet hanging around-until classmate Leonie invites her to convert Winona into one of the gang. It's a tough challenge-but Daisy's determined to try...

You Must be Joking, Jimmy!

Jenny Oldfield

It's school sports day, and Jimmy finds
his teacher's diary. Daisy expects to learn
some spicy secrets, but the diary, like
Miss Ambler, is DULL! So Daisy invents some
more exciting entries. Jimmy now believes
that Rambler-Ambler is going out with a
soccer superstar, but the rest of the
class are suspicious. Can Daisy
convince them it's true?